Jack Frost

A Movie Storybook by Jane Mason
Based on the screenplay by Mark Steven Johnson and Steven Bloom & Jonathan Roberts

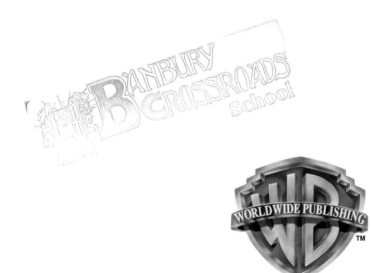

WORLDWIDE PUBLISHING
™

SCHOLASTIC INC.

New York Toronto London Auckland Sydney Mexico City New Delhi Hong Kong

ISBN 0-590-66070-5

Designed by: Lorraine Forte

TM & © 1998 Warner Bros.
Published by Scholastic Inc.
Scholastic and associated logos are trademarks and/or registered trademarks of Scholastic Inc.
Printed in the U.S.A.
12 11 10 9 8 7 6 5 4 3 2 1   8 9/9 0 1 2 3/0
First Scholastic printing, December 1998

In Medford, Colorado, Charlie Frost closed his textbook and raced out the door. Finally, Christmas vacation! But just over the ridge near the schoolyard, a group of his friends was getting pummeled with snowballs. Seventh-grade bully Rory Buck was in charge of the assault.

"Eat snow, you little wieners!" Rory shouted as he pitched a giant snow boulder at the younger kids.

Charlie scowled. Rory was always stirring up trouble. And a second grader named Alexander was caught in the middle of the battlefield.

Charlie had a plan. Using his friend, Tuck, as a decoy, Charlie faked out the seventh graders and nailed Rory in the face with a brainfreeze of snow. Soon Alexander was safe.

Charlie grinned. It was Christmas vacation. He'd defeated Rory Buck. And his *dad* was coming home today!

Waving to his friends, Charlie raced home.

As the leader of the Jack Frost band, Charlie's dad was on the road a lot. But tonight he'd be home for Christmas vacation. Charlie stayed up as long as he could. Soon he heard a familiar voice call his name.

"Charlie, Charlie-boy. The old man's home."

Charlie sat up in a hurry. Yahoo!

Within minutes Charlie and Jack bundled up and were building a snowman in the backyard—a Christmas tradition. Charlie's mom, Gabby, watched from the living room window.

Charlie stacked the snow boulders on top of one another. "Okay, eyes," he said.

Then a nose. A mouth. Two stick arms.

"Hmmm," Charlie said. "A scarf."

Jack sacrificed his scarf for the snowman. "Satisfied?"

Charlie shook his head. "Gloves and hat," he said.

"You are tough!" his dad declared with a grin. But he took off his gloves and hat and put them on the snowman.

Charlie laughed. "He kinda looks like you, Dad."

Later on, Jack tucked Charlie into bed. Charlie snuggled under the covers. "Hey, did you bring me anything?"

"Uh, yeah," Jack bluffed. He'd completely forgotten to buy Charlie an on-the-road present. Flustered, he dug around in his pockets and pulled out one of his harmonicas.

Charlie gave the instrument a skeptical look. "One of your harmonicas?" He was disappointed.

"Hey," Jack replied. "This harp has special powers."

Charlie rolled his eyes. "Yeah, right."

"Really," Jack went on. "Anytime you need me, no matter where I am, you just play on this harp and I'll hear you."

Charlie looked over the beat-up harp. "You just made that up," he said.

Jack gave Charlie a kiss. "Good night, Charlie-boy."

"Dad, I have a hockey game tomorrow. Can you come?"

Jack's eyes lit up. "Yeah, and I can even teach you the J-shot." The J-shot was a special hockey shot that Jack had invented. Suddenly, Jack's face fell. "Actually, me and the guys have to record some songs tomorrow for a big record executive."

"My game's not till four o'clock. It's against our archrivals, the Devils."

"Four o'clock?" Jack repeated. "You know what? I'm there."

"Really?" Charlie sounded surprised. His dad had never made it to a hockey game.

Jack nodded. "I promise."

The next afternoon, Charlie suited up for the game with the rest of his teammates. He wanted more than anything to beat the Devils – to crush 'em! The problem was, the Devils had some really good – and really mean – players, including Rory Buck. Rory's two main sidekicks, Mitch and Pudge, were no fun, either.

Charlie tried to ignore them and play his best. But with the other team playing dirty, it wasn't easy.

Finally, Charlie got the puck. He skated toward the Devils' goal and swung hard. But the puck went way wide, and into the stands.

A second later Charlie was slammed into the glass by Rory. "Nice shot," Rory taunted. "If you're golfing!"

Charlie checked the scoreboard. Mountaineers 0, Devils 3. They were losing, big time.

Charlie looked into the stands. His mom was there, cheering him on. And the other players' dads were cheering, too. But *his* dad was nowhere to be seen.

When Jack got home that night, he knew he was in trouble. An upset Charlie camped out in a tent in his room. Jack poked his head inside.

"How d'ja do?" Jack asked.

"We got slaughtered. Eight-zip."

"Oh, Charlie, I'm sorry I didn't make it. Did you use the J-shot?"

"You haven't taught it to me yet."

Jack sat down. "I need to talk to you about something important. See, I'm chasing a dream I've had since I was a kid. But sometimes it makes me act like a selfish jerk who screws up."

"Are all musicians selfish jerks?" Charlie asked.

"No . . . yes . . ." Jack sighed. "Tell you what, why don't we spend Christmas in the mountains? We'll go to the cabin at Pine Top. No band. No phones. No TV. A real vacation. What do you say?"

Charlie looked excited. "Will you teach me the J-shot?"

Jack tousled his son's hair. "I'll teach you the J-shot. Honest."

The next morning Charlie dragged a giant duffel bag into the kitchen. "What's in there, a body?" his dad teased.

"Walkman, Gameboy, batteries, food," Charlie started down the list.

Just then the phone rang. It was John Kaplan, the big record executive. Great news!

"They loved our tape!" Jack said when he got off the phone. "They're signing us to a contract!"

Gabby and Charlie cheered.

"But they want us to come to a chalet in Aspen. We'll sign the contract and play for John's Hollywood Christmas bash."

"When?" Gabby wanted to know.

"Well . . . tomorrow."

Charlie's head shot up. Tomorrow was Christmas! And his dad had promised them a family vacation in the mountains!

"If I drive straight through, I can be back before Santa's official midnight deadline," Jack went on.

Charlie looked up at his dad. How could he break another promise?

Before long the band had come to pick up Jack. Mac, Jack's band mate and best friend, was driving a Cadillac, and the rest of the band was in a van.

Jack said good-bye to Gabby, but she barely gave him the time of day. And Charlie wouldn't even look at him. He just sat there, fuming. Then he handed over the harmonica Jack had given him.

"Charlie, that's the harmonica I gave you."

"Just take it. I don't want it." Charlie stared straight ahead as Jack sadly took the harmonica and climbed into Mac's Cadillac.

That was the last time Charlie saw his dad.

Winter turned to spring, spring to summer, summer to fall, and fall to winter. Soon it was Christmas again. Snowflakes fell to the ground in Medford as the final school bell rang. Vacation!

Students poured out of classrooms into the schoolyard, shouting and laughing. But this year Charlie Frost didn't say good-bye to his friends, or bother to hurry home.

"Frost! Ya big dinkwad!" Rory Buck shouted after him as he pelted Charlie with a snowball.

"Forget it, Rory," Pudge said. "He's no fun to pick on since his dad died."

"Well, it's time he got over it. I never even met my old man," Rory declared.

Charlie didn't care if Rory teased him. These days, he didn't really care about anything. Not even hockey.

In fact, a few days later on his way home from practice, Charlie cut through the woods to a secret place—a frozen pond. He tossed his skates into the air, and they caught on a tree branch.

No more hockey. No more anything.

That night Charlie watched his friend Natalie build a snowman with her dad and little brother.

Before he could stop himself, he dug an old box out of a closet and pulled a parka on over his pajamas.

Outside, the air was crisp. Charlie set the box down in the middle of the yard and got to work. First, the biggest ball for the bottom. Then the smaller snowballs, one on top of the other. Two stick arms. Three buttons down the middle. Two charcoal eyes, and a cork nose.

Charlie
tore open the dusty
box and pulled out the
clothes — his dad's clothes — from
last year's snowman. The scarf,
mittens, and a porkpie hat. But there
was something else in the bottom of
the box — something shiny.
The harmonica his dad had
given him — the one he gave back.
Slowly, Charlie bent down
and picked it up. He put it to
his lips and blew. . . .

Outside,
the wind picked up.
Snow whirled around Charlie's
snowman . . . faster and faster. All of
a sudden, thunder boomed. Lightning
crisscrossed the sky, and a voice
echoed above the wind.
" . . . I'm gonna be there. . . ."
In the next instant, everything went
still. . . .
And the snowman blinked,
stretched, and took a look around!
"I'm home," he said excitedly as
he waddled to the front door. "Gabby!
Charlie!"
But the door was locked.

In his room, Charlie
thought he heard something outside. He
turned on the light next to his bed and sleepily
shuffled to the window.

"Charlie, couldya get the door?" a voice said. "It's me, Dad."

Charlie blinked and looked out into the darkness. The snowman
had his face pressed to the glass on the other side.

"Aaaagh!" Charlie shrieked. He bolted across his room, turned off the
light, and threw himself under his covers.

Outside in the darkness, the snowman saw his reflection in Charlie's
bedroom window.

"Aaaagh!"

He spun around, but no one was there. He raised his branch arms. He took
off his mittens and wiggled his stick fingers. He felt his body: his head, his middle,
and his giant bottom. He was made of three huge snow boulders.

"NOOOOOOO!!!" he shouted.

Suddenly, the snowman remembered the accident from a year ago. He heard the trickling of liquid from a broken pipe. And that tinkling sound was so real. . . .

Jack looked down and saw Chester, Charlie's dog, peeing on him. Disgusting!

For the rest of the evening, Jack tried to get into the house. But Charlie barricaded the door. He was totally freaked out!

Outside, Jack was having his own troubles. Chester thought his stick arms were for playing fetch, and yanked one right out of Jack's frozen body! Worse, a giant snowplow scooped him up and pushed him down the street!

"Hey!" Jack shouted at the oblivious driver. "I'm walkin' here!"

A second later — SMASH! — Jack's body was squashed face first into a giant wall of snow.

Jack's stick arms pushed against the wall. Pop! His middle snowball came loose and bounced into the street.

"Don't just sit there!" Jack shouted at his middle section. "Gimme a hand!"

The middle snowball came forward to help, and after a lot of struggling, Jack was back in one piece again.

The next morning, Charlie circled the snowman suspiciously. Then he ran into the house and got a hair dryer.

Charlie aimed the hair dryer straight at the snowman. "I know you're alive, so you'd better start talking," he demanded.

"Not the Sunbeam!" The snowman's voice shook.

"AAAGH!" Charlie dropped the hair dryer and ran for his life!

When he was safe in the woods, Charlie stopped to catch his breath. Peeking out from behind a tree, he saw Natalie. Rory, Mitch, and Pudge were playing keep away with her hat. Rory filled Natalie's hat with snow. But just as he handed it back to her – WHAM! – a snowball smacked him in the face.

"I thought you'd learned your lesson, Frost!" Rory shouted. "Guess it's time for a refresher course!"

Charlie looked around, confused. *He* hadn't thrown the snowball at Rory! Then, with a groan, he realized who had.

The snowman!

The snowman's arms were whirling in circles, scooping up snowballs with each turn. "You don't mess with the wizard of blizzard!"

Charlie raced up the hill, grateful for the momentary protection. "Get him!" Rory shouted, pointing at Charlie. A moment later Charlie found himself perched over the edge of a gully – with three bullies right behind him!

"I've got you covered, bud!" the snowman called. He catapulted himself into the air, just in time to catch Charlie.

"OOOF!" the snowman murmured as Charlie landed on top of him on a toboggan.

The two were safe, but not for long. Rory and his thugs were after them on snowboards and sleds. Soon they launched gigantic snow boulders—headed straight for Charlie and the snowman!

Luckily, their toboggan slid into a tunnel before the boulders could hit them. But when they rocketed out the other end, the toboggan began to rip down the middle.

"Time to split!" the snowman declared. With a swift stomp, he broke the toboggan into two pieces, and each rider stood up. Snowboards!

Charlie and the snowman zigzagged through a maze of trees to safety.

"That was awesome!" Charlie exclaimed when they'd finally come to a halt.

"You ain't kidding!" the snowman agreed. "Man, there's an advantage to being built this way."

Charlie eyed the snowman warily. "So, I'm supposed to believe you're my dad."

"Hey, I'm having a little trouble dealing with it myself, okay?"

Charlie decided to give this frozen goon a little test. "If you're really my dad, how did my hamster die?"

"Heart attack."

"Nope," Charlie said. "Vacuum cleaner."

"I bet it had a heart attack on the way in," the snowman joked.

"How'd I break my retainer?"

"You put it in your back pocket and then sat on it at school."

Charlie shook his head. "Trick question. I never had a retainer. What position do I play in hockey?"

"That's easy. Winger. Right wing . . . I mean you *used* to play center but . . ."

"Wrong! They moved me to defense a while ago."

"Aww, really?" The snowman seemed upset. "You were a great wing-man, Charlie-boy."

Charlie's eyes widened. "What did you call me?"

"Charlie-boy."

Charlie gazed into the snowman's eyes and saw his own reflection. Suddenly, he knew it was true.

"Dad!"

They hugged. After a few moments a piece of snow came off in Charlie's hand. He took a step back. "This is too weird!"

Charlie took the snowman home. Once inside, he opened the windows and turned on the air conditioning full blast. Soon the place was freezing.

Suddenly, Gabby pulled up in the driveway. Frost panicked. "She can't see me like this!"

Charlie dashed into the front hall just as his mom came through the door.

"Why are all the windows open?" Gabby sounded annoyed.

Charlie thought fast. "Science fair project," he blurted. "It's, uh, all about what it's like to live in an igloo."

Charlie followed his mom into the kitchen.

"Why is the floor wet?" Gabby asked. She opened a closet — where Frost was hiding! Petrified, he held out the mop for her. Her back turned, Gabby took it and began mopping the floor.

While Charlie distracted Gabby, Frost waddled out the front door. Safe!

The next morning, Charlie peeked outside to make sure the snowman – Frost – was at his regular post. Then he quickly snuck out the back door. . . .

And ran right into him! "I invented the back-door escape, okay?" Frost said. "Where are you going?"

"Somewhere alone, to think," Charlie said. "Since you showed up, Rory Buck wants to kill me, Mom thinks I'm nuts, and I'm pretty sure my dad's a snowman."

Frost was determined to go with Charlie.

Charlie gave in. But since they couldn't let people see Frost walk around by himself, Charlie pulled him on a sled.

"I can't believe I let you talk me into this," Charlie told his dad as people stared at them.

Frost grinned. "I think we look kind of cute."

They passed the bank—where Gabby worked. Gabby looked out the window, and her mouth dropped open in surprise.

Something was definitely not right with her son.

A little while later Charlie took Frost to his favorite place – the frozen pond.

"You know, Charlie," Frost said, "the night I crashed I had turned around. I was on the way back to see you."

"Mom told me that," Charlie admitted. "So, why were you coming back?"

Frost gazed at his son. "Well, I decided that playing music was important, but that you and Mom were more important."

Frost looked up and saw Charlie's ice skates hanging from a tree.

"So, why'd you quit the team?"

Charlie looked away. "Hockey's not that great."

Frost didn't believe him. "Right. That's why the last person you see before you go to sleep every night is Wayne Gretsky on your wall." Then Frost noticed the smooth surface of the frozen pond—a natural ice rink. "C'mon. Let me teach you the J-shot."

Charlie shook his head. "I don't think so."

"Oh, I see," Frost said, standing up. He turned around and belted out an up-tempo, bluesy riff. "Time to get off your big, fat butt," he sang.

Charlie smiled in spite of himself. His dad might be a goofy-looking snowman, but he was still a cool musician. Only he'd never admit that to *him*.

"Okay, okay!" Charlie shouted. "I'll do it just to get you to stop singing."

They played for hours. It took Frost a while to get the hang of it. First he had to adjust to not having any feet. Then his arms flew out of his body. Finally, though, he was whipping the puck around like old times.

"Okay, now," Frost told Charlie, "the trick is to stay relaxed. Keep your arms and wrists straight but loose."

Charlie imitated his dad.

"And instead of just swinging at the puck, pull it back toward you, and then whip it back out like the letter J."

Charlie did what his dad told him. It took a few tries, but finally he figured it out. And by the end of the day he was firing J-shots at the goal like a pro.

The incredible J-shot had been conquered!

"Thanks for showing me the J-shot," Charlie said when they got home.

Frost nodded. "Now I can't wait for you to use it — in a real game. You've got to get back on the team."

Charlie shook his head. "I don't know about that."

"I do. You're letting yourself — and your friends — down. And about your schoolwork. You've got some serious jamming to do."

Charlie couldn't believe his dad — a snowman! — was hassling him about school. "What is this, a lecture?" Charlie almost shouted. "*Now* you give me a lecture?"

Frost didn't back down. "And another thing. I'm a little worried about your mom."

Charlie rolled his eyes. "Why are you telling me this?"

"Because you've got responsibilities now," Frost explained. "You've got to have the guts to face them."

"Hey!" Charlie was really shouting now. "I'm only twelve years old! I . . . I can't handle this!"

Furious, Charlie stomped across the yard and into the house.

That night, Charlie had a hard time sleeping. He had a lot on his mind. He knew his mom *was* having a hard time. He *hadn't* been trying in school. He had been ignoring his friends. And deep down, he did love hockey more than almost anything. But the thing was, he wasn't blowing off this stuff on purpose. It was just that everything seemed really hard. What if he couldn't do it all?

The next morning, the hockey van pulled up across the street to pick up Natalie. Most of the team was inside – Tuck, Spencer, Dennis, and Coach Gronic. Charlie hurried over to the van.

"Hey, guys, hey, coach," he said. "I'd like to come back on the team."

"Are you alone, or do we have to take your snowman buddy, too?" Dennis asked.

Charlie ignored that comment, even though he knew Frost could play hockey better than any of them. . . .

"I say we let him back on the team," a voice suddenly said. It was Natalie. "Everybody deserves a second chance."

Charlie grinned, and a few minutes later he was hurrying out of the house with his gear.

"When do they drop the puck?" Frost wanted to know.

"Eleven-thirty," Charlie said.

Frost nodded. "I'll be there."

The van pulled away, and Frost sagged. The sun was shining, and the air was warm. Colorado was having a Christmas heat wave . . . and snowmen melted in the heat.

"Listen, Chet," Frost told Chester as he grabbed the dog's collar. "You've got to help me, 'cause I've got a promise to keep." He tied the dog to Charlie's sled, then picked a branch up off the ground. "Heeyaaa!" he shouted, cracking it through the air.

Chester took off running, and the sled lurched forward. Now Frost was getting somewhere!

On the hockey rink, things weren't going so well. The game was against the Devils, and Rory Buck was out for revenge. He and his teammates slammed the Mountaineers into the ice, the glass—anywhere they could. As usual, they were playing dirty.

A few blocks away, Frost wrung out his scarf, which was full of water. He was melting fast!

Frost left Chester with the sled and waddled from the shade of one tree to another. Slowly but surely, he was getting closer to the hockey rink.

"Almost . . . there . . . almost . . . there. . . ." he kept telling himself. Suddenly, his eyes widened in horror. There, directly in front of him, was a simmering hot asphalt parking lot. Melt city!

Taking a deep breath, he started across as fast as he could. SZ^{ZZZ}! His bottom sizzled like butter in a hot skillet.

"Hot! Hot! Hot!" he exclaimed. But nothing was going to keep him from Charlie's hockey game.

Inside, the Devils were still playing dirty. But by some miracle, the score was only 1–0. Rory skated by Charlie at center ice. "Give up, Frost," he said.

"Kick their butts, Charlie-boy!" a voice shouted from the bleachers.

Charlie's ears perked up. His dad! His dad was here! Suddenly, he felt unstoppable.

Charlie zoomed past Rory, caught a pass from Natalie, and blasted a monstrous J-shot toward the Devils' goalie. It zipped right by him. Goal!

"Yesss!" Frost cheered. He'd just watched Charlie score his first goal ever!

The game was tied with less than a minute to play. Rory got the puck and skated straight for the Mountaineers' goalie, Tuck. Tuck cringed in fear, but stood his ground. The puck smacked him right in the mask and knocked him on his butt, but there was no goal.

The Mountaineers still had a chance to win! Dennis picked up the rebound

and passed it to Charlie, who passed it to Natalie. She shot, but the Devils' goalie blocked it.

"The ricochet, Charlie!" Frost shouted. "Get the ricochet!"

Charlie saw the rebound. Rory tried to muscle him out of getting the puck, but Charlie ducked just in time. He tipped the puck, and it swished into the goal just as the buzzer sounded.

The Mountaineers had won!

After the game, Charlie found his dad under the bleachers.

"Killer game, Charlie-boy," Frost said. "You rocked."

Charlie smiled — then looked down and saw the puddle at his feet. Frost was melting — fast!

"I've got to get you someplace where it's really cold," Charlie declared. Working quickly, Charlie loaded Frost onto a dolly and burst out the door. Across the street was a truck that had just finished unloading Christmas trees, and was heading back into the mountains, where it was always cold, where Frost would not melt. But as Charlie and Frost neared the truck, it pulled away.

"No! Wait!" Charlie shouted. He pushed the dolly down the street as fast as he could.

Luckily, the truck pulled into a nearby mini-mart gas station. Charlie wheeled his dad up to the rear of the truck . . .

Just as Rory Buck strolled out of the mini-mart.

"You and me, Frost," he challenged Charlie to a fight. "Once and for all."

Charlie shook his head. "I'll fight you any time you want, Rory. Just not now."

Rory glared at Charlie. "I don't know who's stupider. You or your snowman."

"Did you say 'stupider'?" Frost interrupted. *Nobody* called his son stupid.

Rory shoved Charlie aside and saw Frost struggling to get up off the dolly. "What . . . what the heck is it?" he sputtered.

"Not what," Charlie said. "Who. It's my dad."

Rory grinned. "I knew it!" he said. "Mitch and Pudge said I was crazy, but I knew you were alive!"

"If I don't get him onto this truck I'm gonna lose him," Charlie said. "Please, Rory. You know what it's like not to have a dad."

Rory's face fell and he nodded. "It sucks. It sucks big time." He stepped forward to help. "Come on!"

The boys managed to get Frost loaded onto the truck, and Charlie leaped onto the back just as it pulled away.

The truck headed up the mountain roads as night fell. "Feeling better?" Charlie asked his dad as the temperature began to drop.

Frost grinned. "Like a new snowman." He stood up and pushed the tarp at the back of the truck bed aside. A nearby sign read PINE TOP.

"On three," Charlie said. "One, two, THREE!" They leaped off the truck onto a snowy hillside.

"Follow me!" Charlie shouted. They made their way to an empty log cabin nestled in the woods. By the time they got there, Charlie was cold and exhausted.

Frost found a warm quilt and wrapped it around his son. While Charlie rested, he made an important phone call.

"Charlie's fine, Gabby," Frost said. "He's sleeping. He scored his first goal. You should have seen him—it was really something."

"Who is this?" Gabby demanded on the other end of the line. "Where's Charlie?"

Frost ignored the first question, but answered the second. "At the cabin at Pine Top," Frost replied.

Gabby stared at the phone receiver in her hand. "Jack?" she said.

But Frost had already hung up and was waddling back over to Charlie.

"That night you came back," Charlie said. "It *was* 'cause I played on your harmonica. I wished for you to be here for Christmas."

Tears came to Frost's eyes. "Thanks, Charlie," he said. "Thanks for giving me a second chance to be your dad."

Charlie slept until the next morning. When he woke up, he rushed outside just as his mom arrived.

"Merry Christmas, Dad!" Charlie said happily. Right then, the world was pretty close to perfect.

But Frost looked serious. "Charlie, I know why I came back — to say good-bye."

Charlie turned pale. "No! I won't let you go!"

Frost wrapped his scarf around Charlie's neck. "As long as you hold someone in your heart, you'll never lose them."

Charlie's eyes were full of tears. "I love you, Dad."

"I love you, too, Charlie." They hugged, and after a few moments Charlie dropped his hands to his sides, letting his father go.

A breeze stirred as Frost stepped backward. Then a whirlwind began to whip around his snowman body, stripping layers of snow from his shape. It whipped faster and faster, until a translucent human form was revealed.

Jack Frost stood in the center of a whirling mass of snowflakes. And then, in an instant, he was gone.

Charlie and his mom hugged as they watched the snowflakes fall to the ground. Deep down, they both knew that Jack Frost would be with them forever.